# Good-bye, Charles Lindbergh

## BASED ON A TRUE STORY

written by
## LOUISE BORDEN

illustrated by
## THOMAS B. ALLEN

MARGARET K. McElderry Books

*In memory of Harold Gilpin and for Vera, with love*
  *—L. B.*

*To Myron Lyzon King*
  *—T. A.*

The author would like to thank Cindy Curchin, Louise and Eric Secker, Ev Cassagneres, and the National Air and Space Museum for their help in researching this story.

Also by Louise Borden

*The Little Ships: The Heroic Rescue at Dunkirk in World War II,*
illustrated by Michael Foreman

(Margaret K. McElderry Books)

Margaret K. McElderry Books
An imprint of Simon & Schuster Children's
Publishing Division
1230 Avenue of the Americas
New York, New York 10020

Book design by Ann Bobco
The text of this book is set in New Baskerville ITC.
The illustrations are rendered in colored pencil.

Printed in Hong Kong by South China Printing Co. (1988) Ltd.
10 9 8 7 6 5 4 3

Library of Congress Cataloging-in-Publication Data
Borden, Louise.
Good-bye, Charles Lindbergh: based on a true story / Louise Borden;
illustrated by Thomas B. Allen.
p.  cm.
Summary: A farm boy meets his hero, Colonel Charles Lindbergh, when he lands
his biplane in a field near Canton, Mississippi, in 1929. Based on a true story.
ISBN 0-689-81536-0
1. Lindbergh, Charles A. (Charles Augustus), 1902-1974—Juvenile fiction.
[1. Lindbergh, Charles A. (Charles Augustus), 1902-1974—Fiction. 2. Flight—Fiction.]
I. Allen, Thomas B., ill. II. Title.
PZ7.B64827Go   1998
[E]—dc21
97-11542
CIP   AC

## *Author's Note*

This book is based on a true story that took place on a farm near Canton, Mississippi, in the spring of 1929.

Charles A. Lindbergh became an instant national hero after his historic nonstop flight from New York to Paris on May 21, 1927. In an attempt to avoid crowds and publicity, Lindbergh often stopped to spend the night in out-of-the-way places as he crisscrossed the country during various flights. On this particular trip, Colonel Lindbergh was flying back to New York City from Mexico to attend the funeral of Myron T. Herrick, the U.S. ambassador to France. Mr. Herrick had befriended Lindbergh upon his famous landing in France. He even loaned Charles Lindbergh his pajamas to sleep in that night.

Harold Rea Gilpin, a Mississippi farm boy, was crossing his pasture on a white horse when he saw a plane. He watched Lindbergh circle his father's farm and then land in a neighbor's clearing. Later, as a Marine in World War II, Gilpin met Charles Lindbergh on an airfield in San Diego, California. Lindbergh remembered meeting the boy on the white horse on the rainy night he had spent in a Mississippi pasture, many years before.

In 1929, on an ordinary day, in a Mississippi field, something big happened.
And Gil Wickstrom was there to see it.
It was just before supper,
and Gil was in a hurry . . .
late on an errand for his mother.
The air felt heavy and smelled of rain.
It was April, sure enough.

Gil was riding old Princess, a white mare.
And he was riding bareback.
He always left his father's smooth black saddle
hanging on its hook in the barn,
because, as he told his sister, Molly,
it was a Kentucky saddle.
And Kentucky saddles were for old men.

Gil and Princess crossed the big creek,
its banks green with willows and cottonwoods.
"Giddi-yup, old girl!"
They cantered up the hill to the back pasture
of the Wickstrom farm.

Then Gil heard the airplane.
There it was, right above him,
small and dark against the pewter sky.

A *plane!* A *real* plane!

It was a biplane, Gil could tell.
The double orange wings were as flat as barn boards.
And the fuselage was blue,
with a propeller and a tail.

A plane! . . . a *real* plane! Smack-dab over his father's fields.
Gil listened to the steady drone of the engine.
He felt his own heart *pump-pumping* against his chest,
just as loud as the engine.

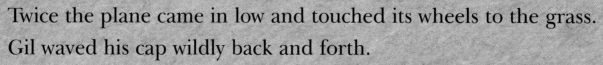

Twice the plane came in low and touched its wheels to the grass.
Gil waved his cap wildly back and forth.
Then the plane was up again, looking for a better spot to land.

Gil lost his smile as the small plane
hummed on across the tall pines.
*Darn!*

Gil pressed his heels to his white mare
and forgot all about getting the laundry for his mother
from Miss Maggie's house, a field away.

"Giddi-yup, Princess!"

Wouldn't that be *something,* to fly a plane across the sky?
To see it all from the air. . .
his father's long fields of cotton . . .
his family's house and barn . . .
even the Pearl River where he hooked catfish
with his friend Artie Meade?

Wouldn't that be *something,*
to wave to his family on their farm,
to his teacher in the schoolyard?
To fly above the Canton town square?
To see all the big places he knew made small?

"Giddi-yup, Princess!"

Gil pressed his heels to his horse once again.
He galloped through the pine woods,
following the drone of the plane.
The pilot would come down by Mr. Meade's big hay shed.
There was a large open space there.
That's where the biplane would land.
Gil knew it, sure as Kentucky saddles were made for old men.

"Gee-yup, old girl!"

And then Gil and his horse were out of the timber
and into the clearing. The biplane had just landed,
bumping its wheels through the tall grass.
The pilot made a wide sweep of a turn
and shut off his engine.
Low voices filled the silence of the field.

Artie Meade and his father were there already.
So were old Mr. Boyd and Henry Galloway,
neighbors from up the road.
They had seen the plane overhead
and hurried to the field.
They had heard it land, and had come to look too.

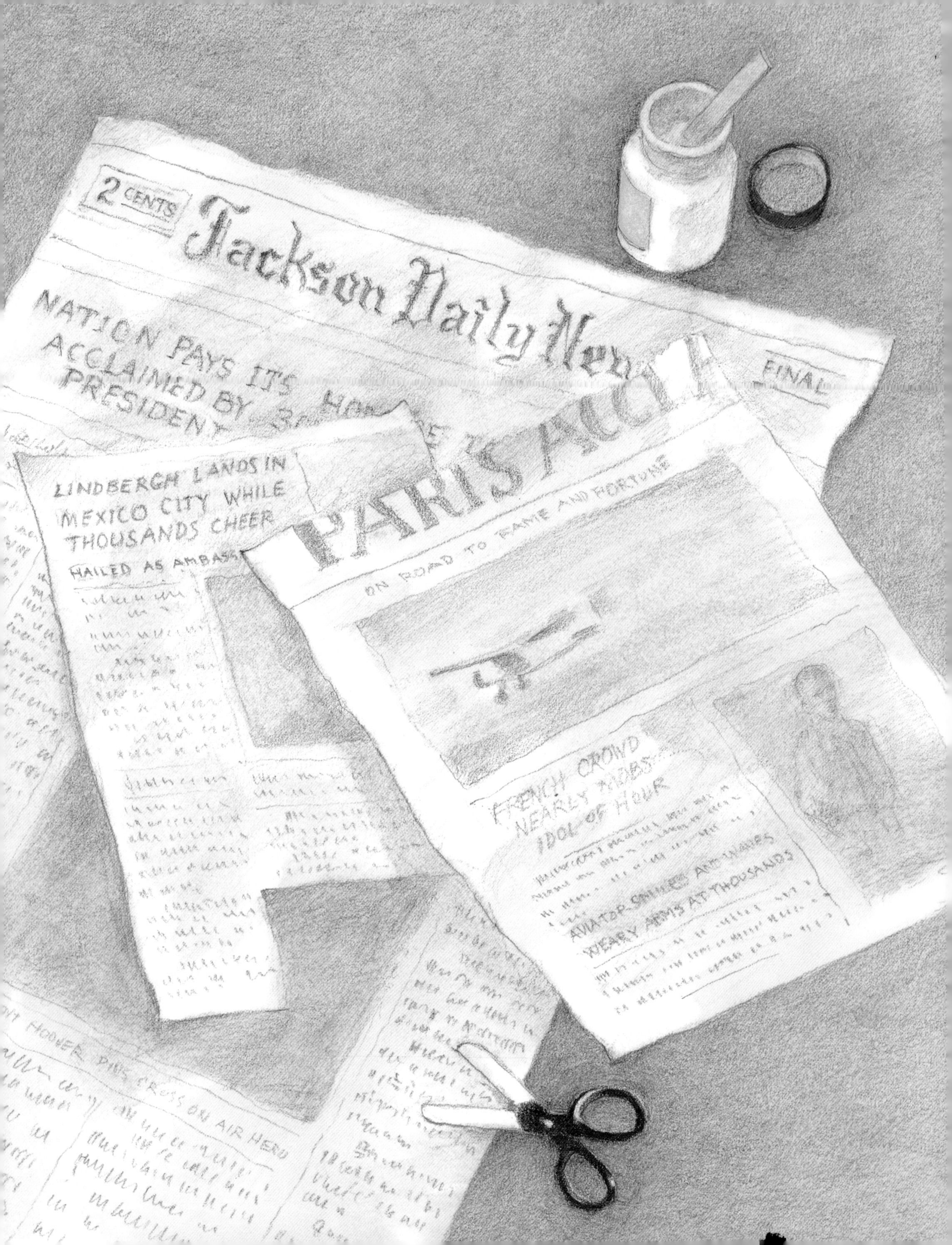

**2 CENTS**

# Jackson Daily News

**FINAL**

NATION PAYS ITS HOMAGE
ACCLAIMED BY 300...
PRESIDENT...

LINDBERGH LANDS IN
MEXICO CITY WHILE
THOUSANDS CHEER

HAILED AS AMBASS...

## PARIS HAIL...

ON ROAD TO FAME AND FORTUNE

FRENCH CROWD
NEARLY MOBS
IDOL OF HOUR

AVIATOR SMILES AND WAVES
WEARY ARMS AT THOUSANDS

...NT HOOVER PINS CROSS ON AIR HERO

Gil Wickstrom had never seen a plane up close.

Only in pictures on the pages of *The Jackson Daily News*.

Even so, Gil knew an awful lot about airplanes.

When he wasn't fishing or trapping with Artie,

Gil had his nose in the newspapers . . .

scanning bold headlines about the country's aviators

and the wonderful airplanes they flew.

He read and reread all the stories about

brave pilots who flew the mail from city to city,

barnstormers who crisscrossed the country . . .

who did stunts with their planes

and walked on wires and wings.

Gil could name all the fliers who had set records . . .

heroes like Charles A. Lindbergh.

He'd flown *The Spirit of St. Louis*

nonstop from New York to Paris.

All by himself.

Gil walked Princess around the biplane three full times,
close enough to touch the sleek orange wings.
He couldn't get enough of that plane.
It was modern. It was fast.
It had come from miles away.
*Curtiss Falcon* was lettered across the tail.
The air was thick with the smell of oil, engine,
and leather seats open to the sky.
Not like a newspaper picture at all.
This was the real thing.

The pilot was tall and slim, much younger than the men
who crowded about the plane.
His brown flying suit was full of wrinkles.

A long chin strap dangled from his leather helmet.
*Where have you come from?* Gil wanted to ask.
*Where are you headed?*

"Would you be Colonel Lindbergh?"
Artie Meade's father was talking to the pilot
in his soft Mississippi drawl.

*Colonel Lindbergh . . . Colonel Lindbergh . . .*
Mr. Meade's words were loud against the quiet of the field.
Gil blinked and nudged Artie. Artie nudged him back.
Charles A. Lindbergh . . . here in this field!
No one at school would believe this!

The famous flier kept his answer to himself.

Then he patted Princess on the rump.

"A fine horse you've got there."

He handed Artie a pamphlet with pictures
about his 1927 flight.

"I sure wish I had one for each of you, boys."

Gil took a step and stood next to Artie.

He touched the pamphlet about *The Spirit of St. Louis*.

It was as real as the orange wing of the plane.

Oh, to be Artie Meade, and have that pamphlet to keep!

Lindbergh's words were low and shy.

Gil knew how he felt.

It was like reading out loud in school
when the whole class was listening.

Colonel Lindbergh pulled off his helmet and began
to set up a small pup tent under the wing of his plane.
John Meade cleared his throat.
"It would be an honor, Sir, to have you to supper at our house.
And we have a good bed in our spare room."

Lindbergh shook his head.
"Thank you for your kindness, but I'm an outdoor sort.
I'd best bed down by my plane."

Henry Galloway stepped forward.
"Then we'll bring you some warm supper."

Old Mr. Boyd looked up at the gray clouds.
"It looks like you're in for some Mississippi rain."
He whispered to the boys,
"Don't start pestering him with questions.
The poor man gets enough from the newspaper people."

Questions! Gil had so many inside,
a dozen wouldn't have been enough to ask.

But the sun was going down, and he'd catch a talking-to
for not getting the laundry for his mother.
Mr. Meade put a hand on Princess.
"Gil, you'll be late for supper,
and Colonel Lindbergh wants his rest.
Your Mama will be calling you across every field."

That night, Gil's mother fussed about the laundry.
And she shook her head when Gil told her about
the *Curtiss Falcon* that had landed in Mr. Meade's field.
"Charles Lindbergh, my foot!
Probably he's just a barnstormer from Jackson
come to scout the 'gators in John's swamp.
And that's what your father would say, too, if he were here
instead of up in Memphis at Aunt Nell's.
Charles Lindbergh would pick a fancier spot
to spend the night than by John Meade's hay shed!"

But Gil's sister, Molly, wasn't so sure.
Her brother knew a lot from the newspapers.
She poked Gil and whispered,
"You can have my rice pudding
if you take me to see that plane."
Gil could hardly swallow his own dessert, much less two.
He had met Charles A. Lindbergh, the man who had flown
nonstop from New York to Paris . . . all by himself.

Old Mr. Boyd was right.
In the middle of the night,
the rain came down in sheets and buckets.
April thunder rolled across the cotton fields.
Lightning lit up the barn and fences clear as day.
Gil Wickstrom couldn't sleep a wink.
He figured Colonel Lindbergh's tent
must be flapping like a shirt on a clothesline.
Rain. Thunder. Rain.
Lightning. Thunder. Rain.
Gil crossed his fingers. He hoped that blue biplane
wouldn't float away.

The fields were dark in the gray morning as
Gil and Molly rode double on Princess,
with a napkin full of warm biscuits with plum jam.
And they were just in time, too.

Artie, his father, and the other men
were already clustered about the *Curtiss Falcon*.
Charles Lindbergh was in the cockpit,
calling instructions above the racket of his engine.
The wheels of the biplane were brown with mud.

Gil joined Artie and the others,
and Molly handed up the biscuits to the man
whose face she had seen in *The Jackson Daily News*.
"Good-bye, Mr. Lindbergh!"
*Good-bye . . . Good-bye . . .*

The colonel called back to Gil,
"Take care of that fine horse, you hear?
Now everyone grab ahold of the wings . . .
Hold tight . . .
And when I wave, everyone let go . . ."

Gil stood shoulder to shoulder with Artie and his father.
All he could hear was the rackety revving of the engine,
a thousand times as loud as the beating of his own heart.
Faster, faster, Colonel Lindbergh's hand turned up the throttle.

Gil's cap blew off, and then Artie's too, in the *whoosh!* of wind.
They blinked their eyes against the roar.
Oil misted the air.
Their hands were strong and tight,
gripping those orange wings . . .
holding the plane back
until Charles Lindbergh was ready to lift it from the field.
Steady . . . steady . . . ankle-deep in the mud . . .
holding the shaking wings of the blue biplane.

Then Lindbergh gave a big wave with his gloved hand,
and they all jumped out of the way, letting go of the wings . . .

The *Curtiss Falcon* jerked past them in a loud rush and a blur. Suddenly it was up, up, higher, climbing higher into the sky, skimming the tops of the Mississippi pines.

Artie ran to get the caps,
and everyone stood next to old Princess,
waving good luck and a safe flight.
The biplane banked and turned east toward Meridian.
Molly said she couldn't wait to tell her friends at school.

Gil waved his cap a dozen times.
"He waved back!" yelled Artie, with a happy grin.
"He waved back just before he tipped his wings!"

Old Mr. Boyd put his hands in his back pockets.
"Maybe . . . maybe not."

But Gil Wickstrom knew,
sure as it was April,
Lindbergh had waved good-bye.